BANANA DREAM

Hasan Namir

pictures by Daby Zainab Faidhi

NEAL PORTER BOOKS

HOLIDAY HOUSE / NEW YORK

For my son Malek,
who loves bananas as much as his baba —H.N.

For anyone who longed for
something they couldn't have —D.Z.F.

Neal Porter Books

Text copyright © 2023 by Hasan Namir
Illustrations copyright © 2023 by Daby Zainab Faidhi
All Rights Reserved
HOLIDAY HOUSE is registered in the U.S. Patent and Trademark Office.
Printed and bound in April 2023 at RR Donnelley, Dongguan, China.
The artwork for this book was created with
digital charcoal /pencil drawing.
Book design by Jennifer Browne
www.holidayhouse.com
First Edition
1 3 5 7 9 10 8 6 4 2

Library of Congress Cataloging-in-Publication Data

Names: Namir, Hasan, 1987– author.
Title: Banana dream / by Hasan Namir.
Description: First edition. | New York : Holiday House, [2023] | "A Neal
Porter Book." | Audience: Ages 4 to 8. | Audience: Grades K–1. |
Summary: Eleven-year-old Iraqi, Mooz, yearns to taste the bananas that
have been made unavailable by warfare.
Identifiers: LCCN 2022033715 | ISBN 9780823451005 (hardcover)
Subjects: CYAC: Desire—Fiction. | Bananas—Fiction. | Iraq—Fiction. |
LCGFT: Picture books.
Classification: LCC PZ7.1.N3558 Ban 2023 | DDC [E]—dc23
LC record available at https://lccn.loc.gov/2022033715

ISBN: 978-0-8234-5100-5 (hardcover)

My name is Mooz.
It means banana in Arabic.

In Iraq, where I'm from,
I didn't like my name growing up when all
my cousins were named Ali and Mohammad.

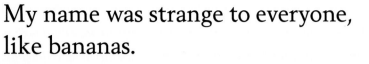

My name was strange to everyone,
like bananas.

We didn't have them in Iraq.
They aren't grown locally because the soil's too dry.

During the Gulf War,
most of the world stopped trading with us.

Bananas weren't available inside Iraq.
They became the forbidden fruit.

Like me, children could only wish
for what they saw on television.

The sight of bananas filled
me with joy.

All Iraqi families received monthly rations:
rice, flour, sugar, beans, tea, and milk.

Bananas were not included.
Bananas were only a dream.

When I was six years old, I asked my mama, "Why did you name me after a banana?"

She told me that once upon a time . . . my parents wanted to have a baby.

The doctors said it wasn't possible.
Mama felt hopeless and sad.

She locked herself in her room.
She didn't want to see anyone.

One day, she had a dream:
she was feeding her child a banana.

When Mama told Baba about the dream,
he was set on buying some bananas.

He traveled for nine hours to the country Jordan,
where bananas were cheap and plentiful.

Two days later, Baba returned with a surprise:
he had brought a lot of bananas home with him.

After eating them for a few days,
Mama was happy and hopeful.

A few weeks later, my parents found out that
they were finally having a baby!

After Mama told me this story,
I had a new appreciation for my name.

At school, I heard the teacher call my name,
and the snickers and giggles that followed after.

But I turned and looked at them.
"I'm proud of my name," I said.

When I turned eleven,
everything changed.

Countries were allowed to trade with Iraq.
Bananas seemed to be falling from the sky.

I had money saved up from
my allowance
when I went to buy
my very first banana.

I smiled and greeted the street vendor.
He was an elderly man, smiling back at me.

"Can I please buy a banana?"
"Sure. What's your name, son?"

"Mooz," I said, no longer ashamed.

I tried to pay the friendly man. "No, son, this is my treat. Enjoy."

Feeling grateful,
I thanked him.
I felt like I was
in a dream.

I stared at the banana.
I slowly started to peel it.

My heart was racing
as I closed my eyes.

I took a small bite of the banana.
It tasted very sweet and mushy.

I ate it in seconds.
All I was left with was the rubbery peel.

And then I teared up in happiness.
I was living my banana dream.

AUTHOR'S NOTE

Banana Dream is inspired by my own experiences.

I was born in Iraq in 1987 and lived there until I was eleven years old. As a child, there was one thing I discovered very early: bananas were a rare luxury.

During Saddam Hussein's reign, most Iraqis survived on monthly rations of the UN oil-for-food program when the world body had imposed trade sanctions on Iraq because of its invasion of Kuwait. As a result, foods like bananas rarely made it into Iraq. We had plenty of apples, oranges, eggplant, tomatoes, onions, and other fruits and vegetables, except bananas. The fruit itself was not grown locally.

We could only watch the yellow fruit on television or dream about them when we slept. When my father drove across the border to Jordan for a business trip, he would bring back bananas with him. Travelers were allowed to bring in fruits and vegetables across the border for personal consumption.

My mother wouldn't let me take the bananas to school with me because she didn't want other kids to see me eat them while they could not.

As we immigrated to Canada, I realized that this once rare fruit in Iraq was plentiful in Canada. It could be found everywhere for little money.

After Saddam Hussein's reign ended, bananas were once again readily available in my home country.

I wrote *Banana Dream* as a message of appreciation and hope.